LUCKY BUNNIES
Diamond's Dream

Hop into
every adventure!

LUCKY BUNNIES

Diamond's Dream

by Catherine Coe

Illustrated by Chie Boyd

SCHOLASTIC

Published in the UK by Scholastic, 2023
1 London Bridge, London, SE1 9BG
Scholastic Ireland, 89E Lagan Road, Dublin Industrial Estate, Glasnevin, Dublin, D11
HP5F

SCHOLASTIC and associated logos are trademarks and/or
registered trademarks of Scholastic Inc.

First published in the US by Scholastic Inc, 2020

Text © Catherine Coe, 2020
Inside illustrations © Chie Boyd, 2020
Cover illustration by Andrew Farley, 2023

The right of Catherine Coe, Chie Boyd and Andrew Farley to be identified
as the author and illustrators of this work has been asserted by them under the
Copyright, Designs and Patents Act 1988.

ISBN 978 0702 30052 3

Printed by CPI Group (UK) Ltd, Croydon, CR0 4YY
Paper made from wood grown in sustainable forests and other controlled sources.

1 3 5 7 9 10 8 6 4 2

www.scholastic.co.uk

Contents

✿ Bright
✿ Burrow

BASIL
FOREST

MIRROR LAKE

PARADISE BEACH

RADISH HIGH SCHOOL

CUCUMBER ROW

HAY ARENA

CARROT CENTRAL

STRAWBERRY FIELDS

**For Julia and Janelle,
two total diamonds xxx**

Not Any Rabbit Hole

This looks like a rabbit hole, right? It's small, round and muddy, with just enough space for a bunny to hop in, burrow around, sleep and eat.

But as you may have noticed, sometimes what seems to be on the outside is very different on the inside. And that's true nowhere more so than here.

For this isn't any rabbit hole. This one holds a special secret. A magical secret.

Inside this rabbit hole is the huge, amazing world of the Lucky Bunnies.

So watch your head, and come on in.

Welcome to the magical land of Bright Burrow...

ONE
Seeing the Future

Diamond sat down on the soft warm sand of Paradise Beach, as close as she could get to Mirror Lake without getting her fur wet. She leaned forward to look into the water. Diamond's reflection floated back at her, her pink eyes blinking, her glossy white head resting in her little paws.

"Hey, Diamond!" someone called from behind her, making Diamond jump. She turned to see Sky and Star walking towards her. Well, Star was walking, with her golden tail swooshing from side to side. But Sky was cartwheeling, flinging up sand with her fluffy blue paws as she spun around and around.

Diamond smiled at her friends, or at least she tried to, but the corners of her mouth wouldn't stop creeping back down again.

"What are you doing?" Star asked, stopping next to Diamond and looking around at the white-yellow sand. "Are you digging for surprises?"

Paradise Beach was known for magical surprises that were sometimes buried under the

sand. Not long ago, Diamond had found a beautiful glow shell that lit up like magic. She kept it on her bedside table at home.

Diamond shook her head but didn't explain what she was doing.

"Ooh, I know!" Sky chirruped, clapping her paws together. "You're going for a swim, right?"

"Don't be silly, Sky," Star said before Diamond could reply. "It's way too cold for that."

Diamond nodded. She wasn't so keen on swimming even when it was really warm and sunny. She seemed to splash so much more than her friends did, and she worried that it might annoy other bunnies nearby.

"So what *are* you doing, then?" Sky kept on, a frown forming across her fluffy blue head. "Is everything OK?"

"I'm fine," Diamond said. "I was just..." She flapped a paw at the lake.

Sky flipped into the air and landed with her back paws in the water. "I've got it! You were trying to read your future! Ooh, I love doing that." Sky peered so close to the water that her

little blue nose got wet. "I think I see something. . . Oh, nope, that's just you, Star."

Star was behind Sky, pulling her back. "Mirror Lake can't really show our futures, you know."

Sky spun around, splashing water everywhere. "Sure it can!" she squeaked. "Last week I saw the biggest, tastiest dandelion cake in the reflection and the next morning my dad had made one. I didn't even ask for it or anything!"

"Well, I can't see anything anyway," Diamond said quietly.

Star frowned. "What were you hoping to see?" she asked, putting a golden paw to her chin.

Diamond sighed and explained, "I thought the lake might show me what my mum and dad are getting me for my birthday tomorrow."

Sky stared into the water again. "Are you sure you can't see anything at all?" she asked.

Diamond shrugged and looked down again too. "Not really, just my own reflection. . . I look a bit small, though, almost like it's showing me in the past, not the future! Definitely no desk for my bedroom. That's what I've been dreaming about for my birthday. I've mentioned it to my mum and dad burrows of times!"

Star put a paw out and squeezed Diamond's shoulder. "Just because you can't see it here doesn't mean you won't get it," Star said. "If you've asked your parents for a desk, I'm sure they'll get it for you."

"Maybe," Diamond said, but she didn't sound very sure.

"So what's the plan for your party tomorrow?" chirped Sky, trying to take Diamond's mind off her birthday present. "It's at Strawberry Fields, right?"

"That's what it said on the invitation, Sky," Star said, remembering the pretty barknote invitations Diamond had given out last week. "It

starts at twelve o'clock." Strawberry Fields was an open-air cinema in Bright Burrow, and all the bunnies loved seeing films there.

"But what film are we watching?" Sky asked, her navy-blue eyes wide.

Diamond's Birthday Party!
12 o'clock
Strawberry Fields
BRING A BLANKET!

"That's a surprise," said Diamond. "I hope you'll like it."

Sky spun on the spot so she became just a ball of blue fluff. "Ooh, I *love* surprises!"

"Sky, we should get going," said Star, giving Sky a look. They'd been on their way to get birthday presents for Diamond, and didn't have much time left before the shops closed. Star wanted to find something perfect for Diamond, but she'd end up with nothing if they carried on chatting like this.

"Sure thing," Sky said. "Or should I say, *shore* thing," she added, looking down at the shore of the lake.

Star groaned at Sky's joke, but Diamond gave her a little smile.

"See you tomorrow at twelve, Diamond," Star said.

Sky leaped into the air and kicked her legs together. "Bye, Diamond!"

The two bunnies waved and then began sprinting away across the beach.

"See you," Diamond replied, watching her friends disappear into the distance until they were just little gold and blue dots. Diamond looked into Mirror Lake again. There really was nothing there apart from her own face glistening back at her, but it didn't look quite right somehow...

TWO
Strawberry Fields

Ruby breathed in deeply as she and Petal skipped towards Strawberry Fields the next day. "I can totally smell the strawberries already!" Ruby said, taking another breath. Her curly whiskers twitched at the thought of the delicious strawberry milkshake she would soon be drinking.

"I can't smell a thing," Petal said. "But I'm very glad I don't have a good sense of smell with all of my brothers at home. I'm absolutely sure that they never wash themselves, ever!"

"Wait for me," squeaked a high voice behind them. The next moment, Twinkle appeared, squeezing in between Petal and Ruby. They looked down at the tiny mint-green bunny and smiled.

"We looked for you," Petal said to Twinkle, "but you weren't at your burrow."

Twinkle nodded. "I know — I was at Basil Forest, collecting things to make this!" He pulled out a beautiful bunch of yellow, white and green flowers. "I suddenly had the furbulous idea to make Diamond a bouquet this morning. It's burrow-tastic, right?"

"It's awesome," Ruby told Twinkle, and gave a long, deep sniff. "And it smells delicious!"

Twinkle pulled it away from Ruby's nose. "Don't go eating it. It's for Diamond!"

"It's a wonderful present, Twinkle," Petal said. "I'm quite sure she'll love it."

They reached the entrance to Strawberry Fields, beside a gigantic stage shaped like a half strawberry. Petal, Twinkle and Ruby saw Diamond near the front of the stage and started to run towards her. She was busy smoothing out her dock-leaf picnic blanket to sit on.

"Oops-a-daisy!" gasped Petal as she tripped on one of her long ears and skidded to the ground right by Diamond.

Diamond put out a paw to help Petal up. "Are you all right?"

"Oh yes, I'm fine!" Petal leaped to her paws and flung her dangly ears around Diamond in a hug. "And never mind me. Today is all about you! Happy birthday, Diamond!"

Diamond smiled, but Petal thought her eyes looked funny when she finally let go. Her smile didn't make her eyes crinkle up like it usually did. Was something wrong?

"Happy birthday!" Ruby and Twinkle shouted, too. Twinkle pressed the big bunch of flowers into Diamond's paws, but instead of looking happy, Diamond burst into tears.

Twinkle grabbed the bouquet back, thinking the flowers had made Diamond cry. "Oh no,

cottontails! Are you allergic? I should have known that! I'm so sorry."

Diamond sniffed as Petal passed her a lily-petal handkerchief to wipe her eyes. "No, I'm not allergic," Diamond said. "Sorry, Twinkle. The flowers are beautiful."

Ruby put a paw around Diamond's shoulder. "Then what's wrong? It's your birthday — it should be your happiest day of the year!"

"Nothing really," Diamond said so quietly it was almost a whisper.

"Come on, Diamond, you can tell us," Petal said, putting her paw around Diamond's other shoulder.

Diamond slumped down to the ground on one of the picnic blankets. "It's just ... my mum and dad aren't coming. And they promised they would."

Petal squeezed Diamond harder. She knew how close Diamond was to her parents. She liked being at home more than she liked being out playing with her friends, even if that meant doing chores!

"Why not?" Ruby asked bluntly. "Are they sick?"

Diamond shook her head. "Nothing like that. They're very well – and happy. My baby brother was born early this morning and they're too busy with him to come today!"

"Oh," squeaked Twinkle. "He must be furbulously cute!"

"He is," Diamond said with a small smile. "And I'm happy, too. It's just ... it's my birthday. I'm a bit sad Mum and Dad aren't here today."

"But *we're* all here," said Petal, "and look, here come Star and Sky! We're going to make sure you have a fantabulous birthday, I promise."

Sky did a backflip towards the group, Star walking beside her. They held out presents

 wrapped in daffodil petals and grinned at Diamond. "Happy birthday to you," Star and Sky sang together.

Diamond looked up, still with tears in her eyes.

"Hey, what's wrong?" Sky asked, the smile vanishing from her face.

"Diamond hasn't had the best morning," Twinkle explained. "But we're going to make this the *pawfect* party. Let's do presents! There's still burrows of time before the film starts."

The six best friends sat down on the dock-leaf

blanket. They put their presents in a pile for Diamond.

"Open ours first," Star said, pointing to the presents she and Sky had brought. "We found the perfect gifts for you."

Diamond reached for the presents with a smile and began unwrapping Star's carefully. But then her face suddenly dropped.

"What's the matter?" Star said. "Don't you like it?"

"It's lovely," Diamond said, holding up Star's gift – a sparkly silver pencil organizer. "I just don't have anything to put it on. . ."

Star put both her golden paws to her mouth. "Your mum and dad didn't get you the desk you've been dreaming of?"

Diamond shrugged. "I don't know. They said my present is at the post office, but they haven't had time to pick it up. My baby brother was born this morning and they've been too busy with him."

"Hey, that's bad luck," Sky said, and then she jumped up to take her present back from the pile.

"What are you doing, Sky?" Petal whispered.

"My present is something for her desk, too!" Sky hissed back.

"It's OK," Diamond said. "I'm happy, really. I have a cute new brother. And my parents promised to make it up to me."

But she didn't look very happy, not at all.

"The same thing totally happened when my little

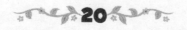

sister was born," Ruby said, trying to make Diamond feel better. "But it didn't last for ever."

Diamond gave a little nod and tried to smile, but her expression looked more like she'd eaten a rotten carrot.

She unwrapped Sky's present – a bright orange desk lamp in the shape of a carrot. Petal's gift was a notebook she'd made herself from bark paper and daisy chains, and Ruby gave her a new bright-green lunch box with lots of different sections to store her food.

Then an emerald-green bunny with long pointy ears leaped on to the stage. "Bunnies of Bright Burrow, welcome to Strawberry Fields. We hope you'll have a berry-illiant afternoon with us! There are just fifteen minutes until

the film begins. Get yourselves settled and I'll be coming around with your strawberry shakes in one shake of a rabbit's tail."

While Sky rolled around with laughter at the bunny's jokes, Diamond opened a picnic basket. She set out the birthday party lunch she'd brought for her friends. There were basil muffins and blueberry scones, thistle tarts and raspberry jams.

"Did you make all this yourself?" asked Star, very impressed with the amount of work Diamond must have done.

Diamond nodded shyly. "I hope you like it," she said.

Sky grinned, her mouth already stuffed with a muffin. "It's scrum-*munch*-cious!"

As they ate, the emerald bunny came around with strawberry milkshakes for all of them. Ruby quickly took a slurp. "Oh, it's awesome. So creamy and sweet!" She kept on sucking up the milkshake, knowing that it refilled like magic whenever a bunny reached the bottom of the cup. They could drink as much as they liked.

The red curtains on the stage suddenly swished open, revealing a huge screen that showed the words *Sing-Along with Peter Rabbit* in big letters.

Twinkle hopped up and down in delight when he saw it. "I've been wanting to see this for ever and ever. It's supposed to be burrow-tastic!"

Soon, the friends were singing along to the film, slurping their milkshakes between the songs. Petal

kept looking over at Diamond to see if she was OK, but some of the time she wasn't even singing. And her strawberry milkshake was left untouched.

When the film ended, the audience clapped and cheered. Ruby lay on her back, rubbing her belly. "I've eaten so much – I'm not sure I can even get up!" she declared.

"Well, we don't have to go yet!" said Sky. "Ooh, how about some party games?"

But Diamond was already cleaning up the remains of the lunch and putting her presents into the picnic basket. "I'm going to go home," she said. "But you should all stay! Thank you so much for coming!" And before anyone could stop her, Diamond ran across the grass of Strawberry Fields.

When Diamond arrived home, the burrow was so quiet she thought it was empty. *Maybe Mum and Dad are introducing my baby brother to some of their friends*, she thought. Diamond began unpacking the picnic basket and looking at the presents she had got.

She nearly jumped out of her fur when her dad poked his white head into the kitchen.

"Diamond, you're home. Did you enjoy your party?"

"Dad!" she yelped. "I didn't know you were home."

"We've all been napping," her dad explained.

Diamond's mum appeared behind him, holding her baby brother. "Would you like a cuddle with Buttonnose?" she asked, lifting the sleeping

bunny towards Diamond. "We named him that because he has the cutest nose, don't you think?"

Diamond looked at his face. *Not really*, she thought. *It's just the same as mine!*

"I'm busy," she said, pointing at the picnic basket. "Maybe I'll cuddle him later." But right then, she wasn't sure she ever would.

THREE
Sleepyhead

"Where's Diamond?" asked Twinkle the next morning as he sped into their classroom inside the trunk of an oak tree. Dandelion School was made up of five different trees – one for each class. Twinkle jumped on to his log chair beside Ruby. Twinkle was *always* the last bunny at school in the mornings ... but not today.

"No idea!" Sky said. "Maybe at home still. She wasn't even awake when I called for her this morning." Sky and Diamond lived in next door burrows and always walked to school together. "And her mum and dad looked *super* tired when they answered the door."

Mr Nibble stood at the front of the class, gnawing on a long stick of celery. *It seems like he's always eating something*, Ruby thought. She wondered whether they'd be waiting for him to finish it before starting lessons. If so, they might be there all day. And Ruby wanted to get going, because the first lesson on a Monday morning was woodwork, her favourite!

At last, Mr Nibble spat out the end of the celery stick, spraying some of the closest students with

his spittle. "Today, we're going to try to make a table out of logs," he explained.

Petal clapped her big pink paws together. "Oh, do you think we could make a desk for Diamond?" she whispered to Star.

Star beamed. "Yes, Petal. I think that's an excellent idea! See, everything with Diamond will be OK. We'll make sure of it."

Mr Nibble showed them the materials they should use to make a table and put them into groups of three. Star, Ruby and Petal were in one group and quickly started making plans for their desk for Diamond.

"Watch out!" Ruby hissed as she saw something white at the door.

Mr Nibble looked over as Diamond rushed

into the classroom. "I'm sorry I'm late," she said to their teacher and passed him a barknote. "This is from my parents."

"I wonder what it says," Star whispered to Ruby and Petal. Unfortunately, Diamond had the best eyesight of the six of them. No one else could see so well that they could read what was on the note.

Petal looked over with wide eyes at Diamond, who'd gone to sit with Twinkle and Sky's group. "She looks so very exhausted," Petal said, wishing she could run over and give Diamond a hug.

Diamond tried to join in as Twinkle and Sky chose logs for their table, but her eyes kept drooping shut and she couldn't stop yawning.

When the bell rang for playtime, the friends soon found out what was wrong. "My brother was crying *all* night," Diamond explained as the bunnies sat in a circle on the dandelion field that surrounded the school, munching on the dandelion flowers. "I couldn't sleep at all. . ."

"Did you try putting your fingers in your

ears?" Ruby suggested. "That totally works for me when my sister's making lots of noise."

Diamond nodded. "It didn't really help. I even tried stuffing acorns in, but then one almost got stuck. I'll probably just get used to it. . ."

After playtime, the next lesson was maths – Diamond's favourite. But she couldn't stop her pink eyes from shutting as Mr Nibble wrote a list of numbers on the chalkboard. By the time he'd turned back around, Diamond was fast asleep, with her head resting on the desk!

Petal looked at her friend, wondering whether to wake her. "It's OK," Mr Nibble said to Petal when he saw her anxious face. "Let Diamond sleep. It looks as if she needs it."

At lunchtime, Diamond came outside with her friends, but she was soon lying asleep among the dandelions, snoring gently.

"We just have to do something to help Diamond," Star said between bites of her tomato and lettuce sandwich. The other bunnies nodded. They were so worried about their friend.

"But what?" squeaked Twinkle. "It's hopping hopeless. We can't stop her baby brother from crying!"

Sky twitched her fluffy blue ears. "I told Diamond she could stay over at my burrow for a few days, but she said she doesn't want to leave home. She wants to be around to help out with her baby brother."

"Diamond doesn't like being away from home, does she?" Petal said. "But it was kind of you to offer, Sky."

"We could make her some extra-big earplugs," Ruby said, desperate to fix Diamond's problem somehow. "I'll work on them as soon as I get home from school!" Ruby started making a list of the things she would need while the others finished their packed lunches.

Having had a long nap during lunchtime, Diamond was much more awake during the afternoon lessons. She worked hard to try to make up for being late for school and then asleep during morning lessons, but she was still behind with everything when the end-of-school bell rang. *And* she had to do her homework!

"Hey, Diamond, are you coming to watch the hop-volley match at Hay Arena?" Sky asked her as they packed up their things.

Diamond's pink eyes lit up for a moment, but then she shook her head. "I'm going to stay here and catch up with my schoolwork."

"Oh, but it won't be the same without you-be-do!" Twinkle told her.

"I'm sorry, Twinkle," Diamond said. "But I don't think I'll be able to get it done later at home. And I need to study for our spelling test tomorrow."

"Well, you know where we'll be if you finish early," Ruby said.

Diamond waved goodbye to her five best friends as they scampered out of the classroom. Mr Nibble was still at his desk, marking some work while munching on cherry after cherry, as Diamond wrote down all the maths problems from this morning in her barkbook.

Diamond didn't realize how much time had passed until Mr Nibble tapped her on the paw. "I think you should be getting home now," he said gently with a cherry stalk poking out of his mouth. "Your parents will be wondering where in Bright Burrow you are."

Diamond looked at the clock on the trunk wall. It was almost eight o'clock! Her mum and dad would have eaten dinner already, and Diamond's meal was probably still sitting on the table waiting for her. She started to panic that they'd be worried about her, but maybe they were too busy – and they'd said themselves just yesterday that she was a big bunny now. Even so, she packed up her school things and rushed out the door.

"See you tomorrow, Diamond," Mr Nibble called. "I hope you sleep better tonight."

"Thank you," Diamond said shyly. She ran home just as the sun was setting, dipping beyond the mountains in the distance and casting a pretty pink light across Bright Burrow.

"Hello," Diamond called out when she opened the door of her family burrow.

At first no one replied, and then her mum appeared, tiptoeing out of her bedroom. Her

pointy white ears drooped with tiredness, and Diamond wondered when her mum had last slept.

Her mum put a finger to her lips. "Shh, we've just got Buttonnose off to sleep – finally," her mum whispered. "It's getting late. I was starting to worry about you. How was your day at school?"

"Fine, thanks," Diamond said. She didn't think she should mention how tired she had been. She wasn't proud of falling asleep during class. And her mum hadn't seemed too upset about how late she had come home.

"That's good," her mum said. She gave Diamond a kiss on the head, then headed back towards her bedroom. "I'll just check that

everything's OK with your brother, and then I'll make your dinner."

Diamond went into her own bedroom to take off her tie. She sat down on her poppy-flower bedspread and leaned back on her fluffy cotton pillow. The next moment, she was fast asleep.

FOUR
Disaster

Diamond blinked her eyes open and stretched her paws above her head. How long had she been asleep? She hopped out of bed and scampered into the kitchen, carrying her favourite stuffed animal under one arm.

"Good morning," her dad said. He was stirring some walnut porridge at the stove and yawning.

"It's morning?" Diamond asked as her stomach rumbled loudly. She realized she hadn't had any dinner last night. She'd fallen asleep on her bed before her mum had even made it. But despite her growling tummy, Diamond felt a lot better than yesterday after a very long sleep. She must have been so tired that she'd slept through all her baby brother's crying!

Diamond's dad nodded. "I made you dinner last night, but we didn't want to wake you. You looked so peaceful. Would you like some porridge?"

Diamond grinned. "Yes, please. With extra berries on top!"

Dad dished up an extra-large portion for Diamond and put the bowl down on the table. But Diamond was looking at something else.

"What happened to my school bag?" she asked, her voice all squeaky like Twinkle's. Diamond's bag was upside down on the floor of the burrow, with her barkpens spilling out.

"Oh dear. I'm afraid Buttonnose got hold of it this morning before we could stop him," her dad said. "I hope there's nothing important in there."

Diamond gasped. "Yes, my homework!" She ran over to her bag and looked inside. The barknotes were all torn, and it looked as if some were missing. "It's a disaster, Dad!"

He hopped over to Diamond to give her a hug. "I'll write another note to Mr Nibble and explain what happened," Dad told her. "Come and eat your breakfast. You must be starving."

Diamond wriggled away from him. "No, I'm not hungry at *all* now!" She grabbed her messed-up school bag, opened the front door and ran out of the burrow before her dad could stop her.

A little later that morning, the bunnies in Oak Class were hopping into their classroom. Sky looked around, spinning on the spot until she became quite dizzy. "Where's Diamond? Her dad told me she'd already left for school. But she's not here!"

"If she left early, perhaps she went somewhere else to get some peace and quiet first," Star suggested.

"But wouldn't she be at school by now?" Ruby said. "Unless she's fallen asleep somewhere."

One by one, the rest of the Oak Class bunnies bounced in, but there was no sign of Diamond. When Mr Nibble took the register, Diamond wasn't there to say yes when her name was called. Mr Nibble looked around the classroom for a moment and then went on with the rest of the names.

By playtime, the five bunnies were all very worried. "Diamond never, ever misses school!" Petal said as she pulled on her long floppy ears.

Twinkle put his hands to his mint-green cheeks. "She must have fallen asleep somewhere. Maybe she's at Paradise Beach or Basil Forest."

Sky clapped her paws. "We'll have to go and look for her at lunchtime!"

"Good idea," said Star with a nod.

The bunnies felt better now that they had a plan, but the next lesson still went very slowly. Petal normally liked history, but today she just couldn't concentrate on what Mr Nibble was telling them about the bunnies who lived in Bright Burrow a hundred years ago.

At last, the bell rang for lunch, and Petal stuck her paws in her ears. It was very loud, and as a bunny with excellent hearing, the bell always made her brain rattle. She ran out of the classroom with her friends, across the dandelion field surrounding Dandelion School's different tree classrooms and out of the gates.

"What now?" said Sky.

"I've been thinking," Star began, "that we should check her burrow first. It'll take us a long time to search all the different places in Bright Burrow, and lunch is too short for that. Plus, if Diamond is just really tired, maybe she's gone back home to sleep."

"And if not, her parents might know where she is!" Ruby added.

So the five bunnies scampered along the blue cobblestones of Warren Street, in the direction of Diamond's burrow.

Sky hid behind Petal as she passed her own burrow. "What are you doing?" Petal wondered.

"I don't want my dad to see me," Sky replied.

"It's a sure thing he'll invite us all in for lunch if he does – and we don't have time for that!"

Twinkle's mouth watered at the thought of Sky's dad cooking them food. He always made the best pies and decorated them so they looked more like cakes! But they rushed past Sky's and continued to Diamond's burrow, where Star knocked loudly on the door.

Petal winced. "You might wake Diamond's baby brother up," she whispered.

Star turned to Petal and shrugged. "But if I knock gently, no one will hear."

Diamond's dad came to the door. His fur was sticking up all over the place, and he had dark circles around his eyes. "Hi, bunnies," he said

in a gruff voice. "Is everything OK? Where's Diamond?"

Ruby thought quickly, realizing that Diamond couldn't be at home then. "We came to pick up some work she'd forgotten," Ruby said before anyone else could reply. "She's busy doing lunch clean-up today." Ruby didn't like fibbing, but she didn't want to worry Diamond's dad just yet.

He opened the door wider. "Ah, OK, then. But it'd be best if just one of you comes in, as Diamond's mum has just put Buttonnose down for a nap."

Ruby looked at her friends and tiptoed in. She pushed open Diamond's bedroom door and looked around for something she could take,

pretending Diamond had forgotten it. That was when she noticed something strange. Diamond's favourite stuffed animal – a little black-and-white penguin – was missing from her bed. She always had it on her pillow!

Ruby rushed out again, beckoning to her friends to follow her as she shot out of the

burrow. "Thanks!" she called to Diamond's dad. He nodded and closed the door behind them.

When they reached Warren Street, Ruby finally stopped.

"What's wrong?" Twinkle squeaked.

Ruby sighed and thought back to Diamond's bedroom and the missing stuffed animal. "I think Diamond has run away!"

FIVE
Lost!

Sky put her paws to her face. "We have to find Diamond. Come on, let's try Basil Forest first!"

"But lunch will be over soon," Star said. "There's no time."

Petal nodded, her long ears skimming the ground. "We'll be in terrible trouble with

Mr Nibble if we're not back for afternoon lessons."

"So we'll have to find her after school, then," Twinkle said. "Is everyone free?"

The friends nodded, their faces serious.

"Hey, I'm sure she won't be too hard to find," Sky said, trying to cheer everyone up. "Diamond never likes to be far away from home."

The afternoon lessons dragged even more than the morning ones. Everyone was worrying so much about Diamond that they couldn't concentrate. The spelling test went badly for all of them, and Star couldn't even enjoy her favourite class because she kept thinking about poor Diamond and how she wished they weren't all stuck at school. She just wanted to go out and find her!

When the bell rang, Sky, Twinkle, Ruby, Star and Petal ran out of Dandelion School faster than ever before. "Ouch!" yelped Petal as she tripped over an ear and somersaulted in the air. Star caught her just before she fell to the ground.

"Oops-a-daisy," Petal said as Star set her gently down on the cobblestones of Warren Street. "Thank you, Star."

"So should we search Basil Forest first?" Ruby asked.

Everyone agreed. The forest was filled with giant herbs of all different types and many bunnies used them for cooking and healing. It was also one of their favourite places to play hide-and-seek. It made sense that Diamond would go there if she didn't want to be disturbed.

The friends ran along Warren Street, then headed towards Sparkle River. They hopped over the silver stepping-stones that were dotted across the shimmering water. They passed

Pineapple Square with its rabbit-shaped clock tower. Twinkle glanced up at it, hoping the Weather Rabbit wouldn't pop out and say it was going to rain or sleet or snow.

They dashed along the edge of Paradise Beach, all looking across the sand to check that Diamond wasn't there, and finally reached the start of Basil Forest. Gigantic leaves in all shades of green, pink, purple and orange waved in the wind. Twinkle stared up at it, with no idea where to start.

Luckily, Ruby had a plan. She took out her list of all the plants in Basil Forest. "I'll go to the east of the forest where the purple silkleaf grows. Twinkle, can you go west to the rosemary and oregano? You're small enough to get through there."

Twinkle grinned. He didn't mind being small — and it was often furbulously helpful in moments like these.

"Petal, why don't you check the north side where the parsley is? You're so tall that you'll be able to see over the plants and check for Diamond easily. And Sky, I think you should try the central patch of mint and sage. I know that mint is one of Diamond's favourite herbs."

Star nodded along as Ruby gave out the instructions. "I'll check the south by the dill and coriander," Star said. "That way we cover it all. Bunny luck, everyone!"

The five friends raised their paws into the air
and shouted, "Bunny luck!"

They all scampered off in different directions,
and Sky headed into the centre of the forest. A
million different smells floated up her nose, but
she tried to focus on just the mint and sage to
help guide her forward. She reached a patch of
wavy green plants that looked a lot like mint and

crouched down to smell them. But they weren't minty at all. She stood up again and looked left and right. Which way had she been going? *Left*, she decided, and started running along again, but then saw Ruby in the distance. *That can't be right!* Sky spun around and hopped in the other direction, sniffing hard. But now she couldn't smell any mint or sage at all.

Sky gulped and stopped by a circle of lemongrass. *I'm not lost!* she told herself. *Just keep going!* She hopped along and saw a little patch of thyme. "What do bunnies have for dinner when they're late?" she said aloud, suddenly thinking of a new joke. "Thyme!"

Sky laughed to herself, thinking she'd have to tell that joke to Diamond later, as she always

found her jokes funniest of all. And then Sky remembered that she was supposed to be looking for Diamond, and that if they didn't find her, she might not be able to tell her the joke, *ever*.

Sky started running, still not sure which way was right. But she decided that going one way was better than none at all!

On the west side of the forest, Twinkle was weaving and winding around the rosemary and oregano plants. He'd found them fine, but not Diamond. He looked around every single stem and leaf, but there was no sign of the silky white rabbit. "Oh furblesticks!" he said to himself. "What now?" Twinkle began scampering away from the plants he'd searched, but now he didn't

 know where to go. They hadn't agreed on where they'd meet once they'd finished searching the forest. Twinkle frowned. It wasn't like Ruby to forget a part of the plan. He'd just have to keep running around Basil Forest until he'd found his friends. And hopefully one of them had found Diamond!

But Twinkle dashed around the towering plants for what seemed like hours. He might have liked being small, but it also meant that his legs weren't very long and running around got very tiring after a while. Not only that, but

the sky was getting darker, and he could see the bright silver moon rising above. He began hopping up and down in a panic. "Oh, cottontails, what should I do?" he cried.

SIX
Bunnies Don't Give Up

"Hello?" Twinkle heard a little voice call out.

Twinkle spun on the spot. "Diamond, is that you?" he said.

A flash of red fur appeared in the distance, saying, "No, it's Ruby."

"And Star and Sky and Petal!" came Star's voice.

Twinkle ran up to hug them all. "Oh, thank burrow!" he said. "I thought I'd lost you all." He looked behind them. "But you don't have Diamond with you?"

The bunnies shook their heads. "One thing's for sure – she can't be in the forest," said Sky. "We've looked *everywhere*."

"We've got to keep searching," Star said. "We can't give up until we've found her."

"Should we tell someone?" Petal wondered. "I'm really quite worried. . ."

"Let's keep looking until nightfall," Star said. "I'm determined to find her."

Sky nodded. "I'm super sure we will! Don't worry too much, Petal."

"Let's run back to our burrows and tell our

parents we're too busy for dinner," Ruby suggested. She wasn't at all hungry, but she knew everyone's parents would be concerned if they didn't go home. "We can say we're working on a school project or something. . ."

"It is kind of like a project anyway," Sky said. "That's not even really a fib!"

"Then we can come back out and search everywhere else," Ruby went on. "Paradise Beach, then Sparkle River. We should try Carrot Central, too!"

Just like before, the friends felt a bit better now that they had a new plan. *Ruby is so good at making those*, Petal thought. They scampered home and, when they were close to their burrows, they agreed they'd each speak to their parents

and then meet on Warren Street in ten minutes. But they were all back at the meeting spot in less than five minutes. They didn't want to lose a second, especially because it was getting cooler and darker. They didn't have very long until they'd have to go to bed.

"Can we stay together this time?" Twinkle squeaked. "I really-squeally don't want to get lost again!"

"I think that's a good idea," said Star. "Come on, let's go!"

On their way to Paradise Beach, the friends checked Sparkle River first. They started at the very end of the river, beside their school, and walked up the length of it slowly, checking that Diamond wasn't tucked into a little hollow or

even swimming in the river itself. There were a few older bunnies enjoying the water – some believed the water helped to keep them young – but Diamond was not there.

At the very north of the river, where it joined the mountains beyond, they crossed a narrow wooden log bridge to get across to Paradise

Beach. The wide expanse of sand was deserted —
with not even one bunny in sight! But Ruby
thought they should cross the beach carefully
just to check. She knew how easy it was to dig a
hole here and hide in it. She'd done it herself
during games of hide-and-seek.

The five bunnies spread out in a line sideways,
holding paws. They walked slowly across the
sand, staring down the whole time so they
wouldn't miss anything. Even if it wasn't
Diamond herself, maybe they'd find a clue!

Halfway across, Sky yelped. The other bunnies
turned to her.

"What is it?" Star asked, running over.

Sky held up a white shell that almost looked
like a bunny face, with two pointy bits on the top

for ears. "It's got to be lucky, right? It looks just like Diamond!"

"I guess so," said Ruby, but she wasn't quite sure how. They needed to find Diamond – not a shell that looked like her!

Sky tucked the shell into her paw and the bunnies continued across the sand. Twinkle sniffed as they reached the furthest edge of the beach. "We're never going to find her!" he said, tears springing into his eyes.

Petal put a paw on his head. "Please don't cry," she said gently.

Star nodded. "We will find her. We're not giving up! Besides, we've still got Carrot Central to check. You know how much Diamond likes carrots – and she must be extremely hungry by

now." Star tried not to think about her own empty tummy. She'd never missed dinner before and it was like there was a creature inside her, gurgling and growling.

The bunnies rushed along the shiny green cobblestones of Cucumber Row, all the while looking left and right just in case Diamond was anywhere here. But all the shops on the street were closed by now, and Cucumber Row was just as empty as the beach.

Star skidded to a halt outside the bright orange carrot towers of Carrot Central. There was almost always a queue outside, since the carrots in the circular field never stopped growing. Every bunny loved this place! But there was no one here, and Star soon saw

why — the gatekeeper was locking the carrot-shaped gates.

"Please!" Star said to the gatekeeper, jumping up and down. "We need to get inside to look for our friend. I promise we won't eat anything!"

The gatekeeper shook her head, making her floppy golden ears bounce around. "I assure you, there isn't anyone inside," she said. "I checked it thoroughly myself. I'd be in trouble if I didn't and locked a bunny in overnight!"

The five friends turned away from the large carrot towers feeling completely and utterly disappointed.

"Oh furblesticks, what now?" Twinkle said. "Poor Diamond!" He thought about his dear

friend hiding somewhere — all alone and cold. They had to find her before nighttime!

But everyone was quiet. Not even Ruby or Star had an idea.

"What's that sound?" Petal said. The friends tipped their ears upwards and listened carefully. Something was scrabbling behind them. They turned and sighed when they saw a black-and-white creature creeping along Cucumber Row in the pinky dusk.

"Not Hiss!" said Ruby, moving one hand to her hip and one to pinch her nose. Hiss was an extremely irritating ferret. He wasn't supposed to be in Bright Burrow — but he sometimes snuck in. And he stank!

"Whats yous doing?" Hiss spat, running right up to the bunnies. "Cans I join in?"

"No," said Star quickly. "You're always horrible to us."

"But perhaps we should give him a chance?" whispered Petal, as kind-hearted as always.

"And maybe he would be helpful in finding Diamond?" Ruby added.

"Whats yous saying?" Hiss growled.

"We've lost our friend," Sky explained. "You could help us try to find her if you like."

Hiss turned up his nose. "Find a bunny? Whys would I want to do that?"

"Because it would be kind!" Twinkle squeaked. "We're incred-furbly worried. . ."

"Wells, I don't care. I thought yous bunnies would be more fun than this!"

Star was about to argue that they couldn't be fun while Diamond was missing, when she heard something else. This time it was more of a squeal.

"Rain is coming!" came the voice in the distance. "Get ready for rain!"

"Nope, nope, nope!" said Sky, stomping her feet. "Not the Weather Rabbit!"

The Weather Rabbit was a mechanical rabbit who lived in the clock tower in Pineapple Square. He was in charge of changing the weather, and

sure enough, a moment later, grey clouds filled the sky above, and huge heavy raindrops began pattering down.

"If Diamond's outside somewhere, she's going to get totally soaked," Ruby said. "This is such bad luck!"

Star turned to her friends. "We have to do something!" She sprinted towards the Weather Rabbit in Pineapple Square, with the other bunnies close behind her.

SEVEN
Soaked!

Moments later, the friends arrived in Pineapple Square. They stared up at the silver Weather Rabbit, who was still outside the clock tower on his mechanical arm.

"Please stop the rain!" Twinkle pleaded, his voice higher than ever. His green fur was already dripping with water.

Sky leaped up and down in front of the Weather Rabbit. "Hey, you have to do something. Diamond's outside somewhere and now she'll be super wet as well as lonely and cold!" Sky's normally fluffy blue fur hung down, all straggly and sodden. She shook her body, flinging raindrops everywhere, but it didn't do much good. "Hey!" Sky repeated, but of course the Weather Rabbit didn't reply. He wasn't a real bunny – just a mechanical one – and he never listened to bunnies' requests to change the weather.

As if to make that clear, the next moment the arm retreated backwards, and the Weather Rabbit disappeared inside the clock tower.

Sky turned to her friends, who were all as wet as she was. Rain dripped from them on to the

chequered pavement of Pineapple Square, making *plinky-plonky* sounds.

"At least the rain has got rid of Hiss," Ruby said, spinning around to make sure the annoying ferret had gone. "That's a bit of luck."

"But we need a lot more luck if we're going to find Diamond," Twinkle said, pulling his little ears with worry.

Petal stared up at the Luck Rainbow, but it wasn't shining at all. Sometimes one strip would shine brighter than the rest, and it meant that a certain type of luck was around. But it seemed as if today was a very unlucky day. She wrung out her soaked ears and shook her sodden tail. Her tummy rumbled, but she ignored it. Finding Diamond was much more important than eating.

"Mirror Lake!" Star said all of a sudden.

Ruby frowned. "You want to go to the lake in the rain? We're wet enough already!"

"I know, but that's where we found Diamond yesterday," Star explained. "She was trying to see her future in the reflection."

Twinkle put a paw to his head, trying to stop

the rain from dripping into his eyes. "But we've already searched all over Paradise Beach."

"But maybe looking into the lake can tell us where we will find her!" said Sky, her hopes rising. "It's worth a try, right?"

Star nodded and raindrops splashed from her head. The bunnies began scampering towards Mirror Lake. It wasn't far, but with heavy dripping fur and puddles dotted everywhere in Bright Burrow, it wasn't easy to run quickly. Plus, the sun had set by now, and they could hardly see where they were going. They hopped across Paradise Beach, the sand flinging up and sticking to their wet bodies. By the time they reached the lake, they looked more like sand monsters than cute bunnies!

Just as they arrived, they heard the Weather Rabbit call in the distance, "Clouds, clouds, go away! Let the moon come out to play!"

"Awesome, the rain's stopped," said Ruby, trying to brush down her wet, sandy fur.

The next moment, the grey clouds vanished from the sky and the full moon appeared again.

"The Wishing Moon!" said Petal, hopping from

foot-to-foot. "Maybe we're getting luckier. Quick, everyone, make a wish!"

The bunnies looked up at the big silver moon and each made a wish. They didn't tell one another what it was, but Star guessed they'd all wished to find Diamond.

"Ooh, look!" Sky pointed further up, to the Luck Rainbow that arced above them. "The yellow strip's shining soooo brightly. Hey, what does that mean again?"

"Future luck," said Star before anyone else could answer.

Twinkle leaped to the very edge of Mirror Lake. "Furbulous — the lake has to tell us our future now!" He peered on tiptoes into the water. "Pleeeeease show us where to find Diamond..."

The other bunnies joined Twinkle, staring into the reflection on the shimmering lake. Star came to look. But all they could see was their own faces looking back at them from the inky water. Sky blinked over and over again, waiting for the lake to show them something. It had to!

Then Ruby gasped, and the friends all turned to her. She pointed at Mirror Lake, but further away than their reflections. Twinkle squeaked and Star punched the air. Sky did a backflip of excitement, and Petal leaned so far forward to look that she tipped over and splashed into the water.

"The Clover Train!" Ruby said, watching it zoom above them in the reflection. The train was

made up of four-leaf clover carriages and flew bunnies all over Bright Burrow. Ruby couldn't believe she'd forgotten about looking there! Not that it would have been easy, because the Clover Train would only stop for a bunny if it had no one riding on it.

Ruby spun around so she could see it in the sky rather than the reflection and wished she had Diamond's amazing eyesight. Diamond could see things really far away — even in the dark!

But still, Ruby thought she spotted something small and white curled up at the back of the Clover Train. She began jumping up and down, waving to try to get its attention.

It dipped down towards the bunnies but didn't

stop. It wouldn't if someone was on it, and there was definitely something on the four-leaf clover at the very back.

Luckily, Star's gran Edna was the conductor of the Clover Train. "Gran!" Star shouted.

Edna waved down as the Clover Train whooshed by them, only a little way above their heads. "Helloooo, bunnies," Edna called. "You're out late! And you're all wet and sandy!"

"I know," said Star. "But listen, we need you to stop. Please!"

Edna shook her golden head, which was so similar to Star's, just a bit wrinklier and with flecks of grey. "You know I can't do that. I can only stop when the bunny who called the train says to do so. Those are the rules."

Star put her head in her paws. Normally, she liked rules, but this was different. If that was Diamond up there, they had to get her down!

EIGHT
The Clover Train

Ruby nudged Star and said, "Then we have to persuade Diamond to stop the Clover Train herself."

Star grinned at her friend. Ruby was right. "Come on," Star said to the other bunnies. "We need to get Diamond's attention!"

And so the five friends leaped up and down

and spun around and around on the beach.
"Diamond!" they yelled together as sand
and water flung from their fur. "Diamond! Is
that you?"

The small bundle of white at the back of the
Clover Train seemed to twitch, just a bit.

"Diamond!" Twinkle squeaked – so loudly that
Petal had to put her paws in her ears. "Please
stop the train! We miss you!"

The Clover Train dipped and dodged in the
air as Edna steered it in circles above them.
She's trying to help, thought Petal. *But it's no
good if Diamond won't ask Edna to stop...*

Twinkle was still squeaking, and now Sky
was leaping up so high she could almost
touch the four-leaf clover carriages. "Hey,

Diamond," Sky yelped as she jumped. "It *is* you!"

Each time she leaped skyward, Sky could see the bunny, and it was definitely Diamond, with her little pink eyes and swept-back ears.

"We've been..." Sky said, before dropping down to the ground again.

"Looking for..." she continued on her next leap.

"You everywhere!" she finished.

"You have?" Diamond said in a small voice as Sky plummeted to the ground again. Then Diamond stood up on the four-leaf clover and called to Edna, more loudly, "I think I'd like the train to stop, please."

Edna looked over her shoulder and smiled. "Good idea," she said, and steered the train towards the beach. Diamond sat down again so she didn't topple over, but she didn't need to worry. The Clover Train kept bunnies on it magically so that no one ever fell off, no matter how fast or bouncy it went.

The train turned in big circles over the beach, floating down slowly until it came to a gentle stop on the sand. The bunnies rushed over to

Diamond at the back, who had her school bag over one shoulder and her penguin soft toy tucked under one arm. They hopped on to the four-leaf clover beside her and all began to speak at once.

"Hey, what happened?"

"We've been really worried!"

"Have you been on the train all day?"

"We've missed you so much!"

"It's furbulous to see you again!"

Diamond's face went bright red with embarrassment. "I'm sorry," she said in the tiniest voice. "I didn't really mean to run away. But once I had, I didn't know what to do. And then I saw the Clover Train, and it was empty..."

 Petal wrapped both her ears around Diamond in a hug. Diamond didn't mind that she got all wet and sandy – she was just happy to see her friends.

Edna hopped towards them across the four-leaf clovers. "Diamond waved me down this morning," Edna told them. "I'm not sure I've ever taken a bunny on such a long trip!"

Diamond smiled at Edna shyly. "I *was* starting to feel a bit dizzy."

"Come on," said Star, reaching out for Diamond's paw. "Let's get off now."

"You must be *starving*, too," added Ruby, whose own stomach was rumbling with hunger.

"I'm so lucky to have you," Diamond said to her friends as they hopped off the Clover Train. Then she turned back to Edna. "Thank you for the ride," she said. The next moment, Edna was steering the train back up into the sky while waving to the bunnies below on the beach.

"Let's get you home," said Petal, but Diamond screwed up her face.

"I . . . I'm not sure I want to," Diamond said.

"But you have to go home sometime," said Star. "And it's extremely late!" She pointed to the sky, just in case Diamond hadn't realized. It was completely black, aside from the shining silver moon, which flooded glittering light across Bright Burrow.

Diamond slumped down on the sand and sighed.

Twinkle leaped over to sit next to her. "Why *did* you run away?" he asked. "Was it because you didn't get the desk you really-squeally wanted for your birthday?"

Diamond shook her head. "No," she said quietly. "It wasn't that at all. Buttonnose tore up my homework. I found it when I woke up this morning. I know he didn't mean to – he was probably just playing. But I didn't want to be at home for a second longer, and it was much too early to go to school. . ."

"Diamond! Diamond! Is that you?"

The six friends spun around to look at who was shouting behind them, and saw two white

bunnies sprinting across the sand. Their fur shone in the moonlight, but their faces looked pale and tired – and very, very worried.

Diamond blinked up at her mum and dad as they rushed towards her. The next moment, they surrounded her in the biggest, tightest hug she'd ever had.

"Oh, Diamond, where have you been?" Diamond's mum asked, her pink eyes brimming with tears.

Diamond tried to reply, but it came out all muffled as she spoke into her dad's fur. Finally, he let Diamond go, and her parents took hold of her paws instead, sitting on the sand with her.

"I-I've been on the Clover Train," she explained with a stutter, hoping she wouldn't be in too much trouble.

"But you're OK?" asked her dad.

"We thought you might have been hurt or something!" her mum said. "Why didn't you come home?"

Petal saw Diamond's dad nudge her mum. "I think we can guess why," her dad said, then turned to Diamond. "I'm sorry we've been so busy with your brother, especially on your birthday."

Diamond looked around, panicking when she realized he wasn't with them. "Where is he now? Is he all right?"

"He's fine," Diamond's mum reassured her. "Our neighbour, Mrs Flufftail, is looking after

him so we could search for you. We've been so worried!"

"I'm sorry," said Diamond, hanging her head.

"No, *we're* sorry." Her mum put a paw around Diamond's shoulders. "We were too wrapped up in looking after Buttonnose. We weren't thinking enough about you."

"But we're going to make up for it now, we promise," Diamond's dad added. "Starting with an extra-special belated birthday celebration for you." He looked up at Diamond's friends. "What do you think? Are you free on Saturday?"

The bunnies grinned. "Yes!" they chorused, and Sky leaped up into the air and did a triple backspin.

A warm fuzzy feeling bubbled in Diamond's tummy. *Mum and Dad do care about me,* she thought.

Star heard Petal sniffling.

"Why are you crying?" Star asked.

"Oh dear, I'm not sad," she said. "Just so happy for Diamond. Everything's going to be all right."

Star gave her friend a hug. "Didn't I tell you that everything would work out in the end? And now we have another birthday party to look forward to!"

Diamond's mum and dad made sure that the belated birthday on Saturday was the best party

the bunnies had ever been to. "Say goodbye to your brother," her dad said as he walked towards the burrow door.

"Where's he going?" Diamond asked.

Diamond's mum grinned. "Mrs Flufftail is babysitting him again – so we can completely focus on you and your party."

Diamond smiled back and reached out to her brother. Her dad passed Buttonnose to Diamond and she gave him a hug. He felt warm and soft in her arms. She breathed in his new bunny smell and suddenly realized how much she loved him. "Bye, Buttonnose," she whispered. "I'm sorry for being jealous before. From now on, I'll be the best bunny big sister ever."

By the time Diamond's dad had returned to their burrow, all five of her friends had arrived. "First of all," Diamond's mum said, "we have your birthday present!" She and Diamond's dad rushed out of the room and then came back in carrying something huge between them, covered in pink wrapping paper and a giant purple bow.

"We're so sorry it's late," Diamond's dad said. "But we hope it's worth the wait!"

Diamond widened her eyes at the present, then turned to her friends. "Will you help me open it?"

They grinned and all six bunnies began tearing at the paper, sending strips flying everywhere. Diamond blinked and blinked

again as the present was revealed. It was the most amazing desk she'd ever seen, with little rainbow compartments across the back to sort her things, drawers with heart-shaped handles and a bright red chair that swivelled and moved up and down. It even had round white fluffy cushions, which looked just like clouds – and they were the comfiest things Diamond had ever sat on. Diamond couldn't believe it – this was even better than the desk she had asked for.

Sky spun on the spot. "Ooh, it's gorgeous! I've never ever seen anything like it before!"

"Me neither," Diamond breathed, staring at her incredible present.

Her mum and dad beamed. "We had it made especially for you!"

"Especially for me?" Diamond repeated. She ran over to her parents and jumped up to give them each a hug. This proved it – they hadn't really forgotten her, not if they'd gone to all this trouble. They loved her after all.

"Oh dear!" thought Petal, and then realized she'd said it out loud.

"What's wrong?" asked Diamond.

Petal's long ears drooped. "It's just that ... we made a desk for you, too!"

Diamond's smile grew even wider. "Really? That's so lovely of you. Two desks are even better than one!"

Twinkle was stroking the desk's heart-shaped handles, oohing and aahing. "How furbulously lucky it has all your favourite things and all your favourite colours!"

Diamond turned to her friend and smiled wider than she had in a very long time. "I don't think that was luck," Diamond said. She knew her parents must have spent ages picking out everything for the desk. "But I do *feel* very lucky – to have parents and friends who love me so much."

And no bunny could disagree with that!

You're in luck!

**Read on for a sneak peek
at what the hoppiest, floppiest,
pluckiest, luckiest bunnies around
are getting up to next!**

ONE
Wishing for Snow

Ruby breathed in deeply as she cleaned her brand new, shiny red ice skates with a fern cloth. She loved the smell of new shoes, and these were extra special – she'd wanted them for ages before her parents had bought them for her birthday. All Ruby needed now was for it to get cold and icy enough for Mirror Lake to freeze over so she could use them!

It had been warm and sunny recently, but with the Weather Rabbit, that could change in an instant. The Weather Rabbit was a mechanical creature who lived in the clock tower in Pineapple Square. He was in charge of changing the weather, and so far he'd never listened to Ruby nor any of her friends when they'd asked him to change it. Ruby knew it wouldn't be worth trying, even though she wanted it to snow SO badly!

With a sigh, she laid the red ice skates back in their box, fastened the lid and put it back in the cupboard. Beside it sat her stripy bobble hat and matching mittens. She tugged the hat over her long red ears and pulled the mittens on to her paws. Ruby looked in the mirror beside the cupboard and beamed. She loved the winter and all the warm, fluffy clothes that went with it.

Ruby wouldn't just go ice-skating, she'd also make snow bunnies ... and go sledging and...

Before she forgot anything, Ruby ran to her bedroom, pulled off one of the mittens and started a new list in her notebook:

Ruby's list of must-do winter things:

- *Ice-skating on Mirror Lake*
- *Building snow bunnies*
- *Sledging down Strawberry Fields*
- *Having a snowball fight*
- *Making snow burrows*

Ruby twiddled her barkpen around in her paw as she thought hard in case she'd missed something. She stopped when she heard a knock at the burrow door. Her parents were out shopping on Cucumber Row, taking Ruby's little sister, Squeak, with them, so Ruby rushed to the door to answer it.

She pulled it open and smiled. A very blue fluffy bunny was standing on the doorstep.

"Hi, Sky!" Ruby said, and beckoned her friend inside.

But Sky stood on the spot, staring at the top of Ruby's head. "Hey, are you OK, Ruby?" Sky asked in her chirpy voice. "Do you have a cold or something?"

Ruby frowned for a moment, wondering

what Sky was talking about, until she remembered the bobble hat and mitten she was still wearing. "Oh no, I'm totally fine!" She whipped off the hat and grinned. "I was just trying them on."

Sky looked behind her, still feeling confused. Bright Burrow was filled with warm sunshine, and there wasn't a cloud in the sky. "I don't think you'll need those today!"

"I know," Ruby replied. "But I just can't wait for it to snow so I can use my new ice skates. Do you want to see them?"

Sky did a backflip. "Sure thing! Are these the ones your parents got you for your birthday?"

Ruby nodded as she led Sky to the cupboard and took the box out carefully.

"What's an ice skate's favourite greeting?" Sky asked with a grin.

Ruby twitched her whiskers, trying to think of an answer to Sky's joke. "Good skating?" she guessed, although it didn't sound very funny.

"No," said Sky. "Have an ice day!"

Ruby giggled at Sky's joke as she lifted the ice skates out of the box. Sky oohed and aahed at the beautiful red skates. "They're super good!" she said, stroking one with her fluffy blue paw. "No wonder you can't wait to skate in them. I'm sure the Weather Rabbit will make it snow soon."

"I hope so!" Ruby said, thinking about the list she'd made of all the fun things she and her friends could do.

"Are you ready to leave for the match?" Sky asked. She, Ruby, and their four best friends were going to Hay Arena to watch a bunny basketball game. They were even more excited than usual because Petal's mum was playing!

"Let me just put the skates away." Ruby laid them back in the box and shut the cupboard. Then she scribbled a quick note for her parents on a piece of bark paper so that they knew where she was when they got home. "All right, I'm ready!"

Sky spun on her toes, suddenly just a blur of blue fur. "Let's go!" she said, jumping up and punching the air.

TWO
Bunny Basketball

Sky, Ruby, Petal, Star, Twinkle and Diamond sat on one of the haystacks at the front of Hay Arena. Petal's mum had arranged for it to be reserved for them so they could see her playing up close. Twinkle swung his legs back and forth as he perched on the hay bale, clapping his mint-green paws. "This is going to be furbulous!" he said.

The rest of the friends clapped as the bunny basketball players ran on to the court, and Petal whooped with delight when she saw her mum. Petal's mum was even taller than Petal, with the same pink fur and extremely long, droopy ears — but she'd tied them back into a bow for the match.

"Go, Lucky Whiskers!" Petal shouted to the team, and her mum smiled and waved at Petal and her five best friends.

Soon the bunny referee blew her whistle and the match began.

"I want to be a basketball bunny when I grow up," Star said as they watched the other team, the Longtails, hit the side of the hoop. "I can definitely bounce high enough!"

Her friends nodded as Lucky Whiskers began attacking at the other end of the court. Star was always chosen for the Bounce-a-Lot event every year and practised jumping without fail every day.

One of the Lucky Whiskers' players passed the ball to Petal's mum, who leaped towards the hoop ... for a slam dunk.

The bunny friends jumped up and cheered. "Well done, Mum!" Petal yelled, hoping her mum would hear her.